The Gnome in My Home

Written by Kim Bridges and Illustrated by Kellie Davies

Dedicated to my family and all who love garden gnomes and all things magical.

-K.D.

To all the little people who spread their magic in such big ways.

-KJB

"Well, it's not the most beautiful burrow on the block," Rabbit said, standing in front of the abandoned hole, "but I suppose it will have to do."

His feet were sore and tired from hopping all the way from Farmer Brown's. "I've been chased with a pitchfork for the last time," he said.

Rabbit sniffed the air inside the dingy dugout. Cobwebs crowded the corners. Dust riddled the rafters. He twitched his whiskers and let out a sneeze. "Oh dear, oh dear," he said, shaking his head. "My, my, my. How I wish I had a bit of magic. I'd tidy up this place in no time. But there's no such thing as magic."

Rabbit sighed, remembering how lonely it had been in his old hole under the Juniper bush, and how hungry he'd been trying to snatch bits of cabbage and celery from Farmer Brown's garden. *At least it looks safe here*, he thought.

Just then there was a bump outside the door. Rabbit popped his head out of the dim burrow and rubbed his eyes. There, at the gate, stood the strangest little garden gnome you ever saw - still as a statue, with a pointy hat and white beard. "Wherever did you come from?" Rabbit asked, his eyes darting from side to side.

Rabbit's nose twitched nervously as he crept closer. Suddenly, the little gnome tipped his hat and said, "Nimble Gnome, atcher service, sir." Rabbit was so startled he nearly leapt into the hedge. The little gnome chuckled, pressing a knuckle to his lips, and said, "I heard ye'd be needing a bit o' magic and I come as fast as I could." Rabbit cocked his head and perked up both ears. "But *where* did you come from?" he asked.

"No time ter explain, laddie. Now, you best move aside whiles I get to work," Nimble said with a wink.

In a flash he tidied the front yard and gardens, then rushed inside leaving a cloud of dust behind him.

Old Badger heard the commotion and came to see what was up. "I- I don't know where he came from," Rabbit sputtered, scratching his head.

"Well, you've got yourself a right lucky garden gnome, it seems," said Badger. "Magical creatures, they are. Hey, everyone! Come quick and see."

Soon the neighbors had all gathered at Rabbit's new home.

Squirrel, Badger, Chipmunk, Goose, and Hare all crowded

around the window to take a peek at the strange little man.

Nimble darted around the house, sparks of magic flying from his fingers. In no time, he'd polished the lamps, lit the candles, carved a table and chairs, woven a rug, whipped up some honey nog, and even baked some tasty treats.

When all was ready, the door was flung open and a delicious smell floated out to all the friends and neighbors.

"Come," said the gnome. "Let's get this welcome party off to a proper start."

With that, everyone piled in. "What a fine place you've got here," said Badger.

"Yes, very fine indeed," agreed Hare, patting Rabbit on the back.

I suppose it rather is, Rabbit thought, feeling quite pleased.

In the light of the afternoon sun, the friends sipped their nog and nibbled their treats. "Let's have some music," Nimble called out when they'd all finished eating. Rabbit thumped a tune with his wide feet and everyone clapped along, watching the happy little gnome dance a jig around the room.

Soon everyone was dancing. "A toast to Rabbit's good health," Badger said, lifting his glass.

"Three cheers for Rabbit," they all cried, "Hip, Hip, Hooray."

Rabbit smiled. His heart filled with pride. *At last, no more running*, he thought. *I've finally found a home and some fine new friends to share it with.*

As the dim light of evening settled on the hillside, Bluebird chirped to Chickadee, "This has been a splendid party, but night is coming and I must fly home to my oak tree."

"Yes," squeaked Chipmunk. "My old stump is calling."

"I must head back to my nest in the marsh grass by the pond," honked Goose.

"Rabbit, you have been a marvelous host," said Badger, clasping Rabbit by the hands. "Welcome to our neighborhood."

"Thank you," Rabbit said, brimming with joy. "Drop by anytime."

Gradually, the friends excused themselves and made their way home. Nimble was the last to leave. "Won't you stay the night?" Rabbit called from the gate.

"Thank ye, but no. I'm afraid I must go. You'll be feeling snug as a bug here now, I'd wager. And if ye ever need a bit o' magic again, well, ye knows what to do." Then, with a funny giggle and a click of his heels, the gnome was gone.

The years have passed happily for Rabbit and his friends. Every now and again, from the corner of his eye, Rabbit thinks he sees the flash of a red cap darting around the corner. Maybe you've seen it too, if you've ever wished for a little magic to brighten your day. Or maybe you're like Nimble Gnome, spreading magic wherever you go.

Whatever the case, next time there's a tasty treat waiting for you at the table, your bed has been made, or your socks folded neatly and set in your drawer, you can be sure someone magical has paid you a visit.

Meet the Author

Kim Bridges has been writing stories since she could hold a pencil. She loves gardening and bunnies - she used to have a pet one named Whiskers. Kim also enjoys swimming, dancing (sometimes a jig), playing the violin, and reading ALL kinds of books. Though she has never owned a garden gnome, she certainly wouldn't mind one paying her a visit someday. Kim lives with her husband and five children in northern Virginia. This is her first picture book. Visit her at: kjbridges.com.

Meet the Illustrator

Kellie Davies has always loved art and illustrating. She loves nature, animals, and fairytale creatures. Kellie contrived *The Gnome in My Home* while growing up in the countryside of north-western Virginia - where many rabbits and the neighbor's garden gnome statues inspired this story. Kellie currently loves to travel the world and brings her art and illustrations wherever she goes. Find Kellie Davies on Facebook: @PaintAndMotion.

Made in the USA
Monee, IL
07 December 2021

84167988R00026